First published in Great Britain in 2018 by Andersen Press Ltd.,
20 Vauxhall Bridge Road, London SW1V 2SA.
Copyright © Qian Shi, 2018.
The right of Qian Shi to be identified as the author and
illustrator of this work have been asserted by her in accordance
with the Copyright, Designs and Patents Act, 1988.
All rights reserved.
Printed and bound in China.
First edition.
British Library Cataloguing in Publication Data available.
ISBN 978-1-78344-536-3

THE WEAVER

Qian Shi

Andersen Press

All spiders lead a life of adventure.

Once they are born, they wave goodbye to each other and catch a lift on the wind.

When the wind drops them off,
they set about weaving a web.

Stanley has found
his perfect spot.

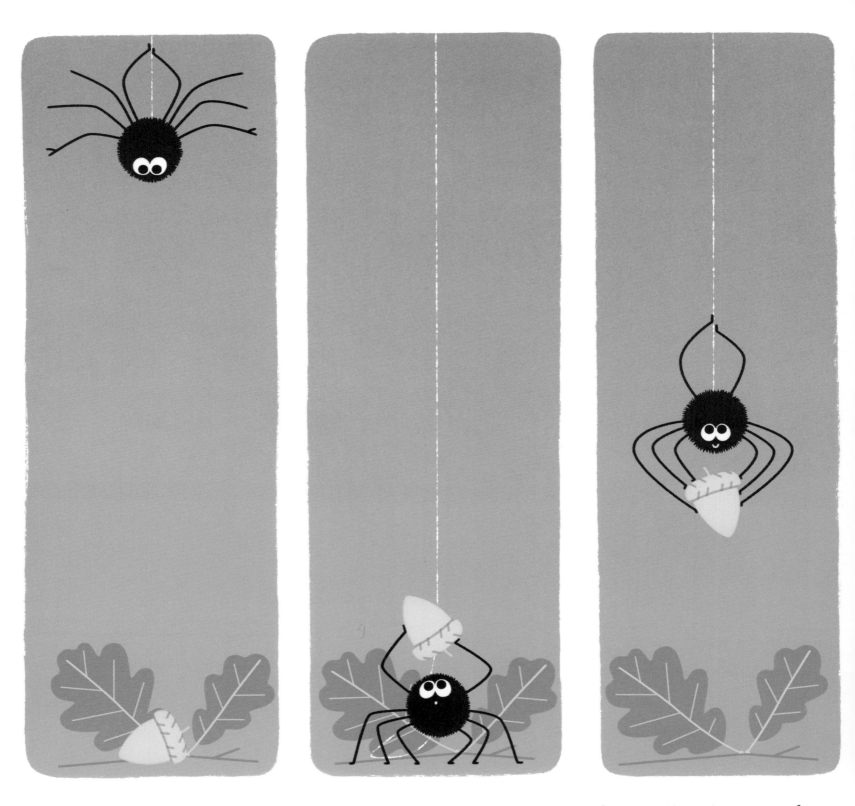

Stanley is a weaver, he is also a collector. He collects seeds,

twigs, leaves...

and all kinds of precious things
he cannot name.

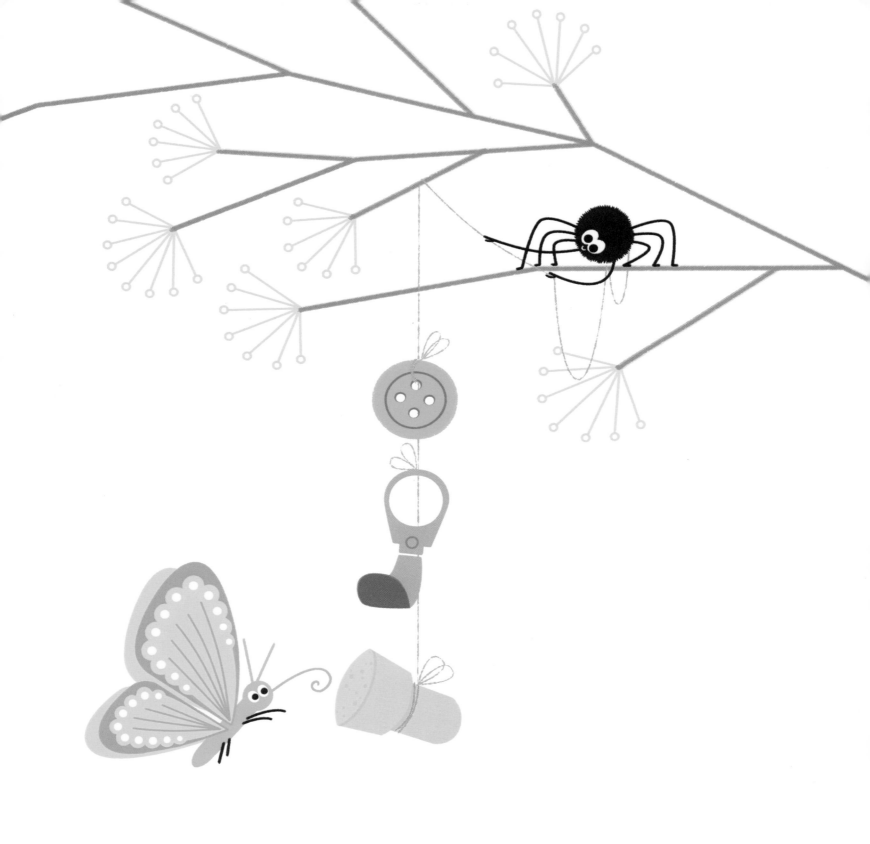

Stanley is very proud of his collection.

But then the rain comes.

Suddenly,
his home collapses!

He only manages to save one leaf.

How can Stanley keep his leaf safe?

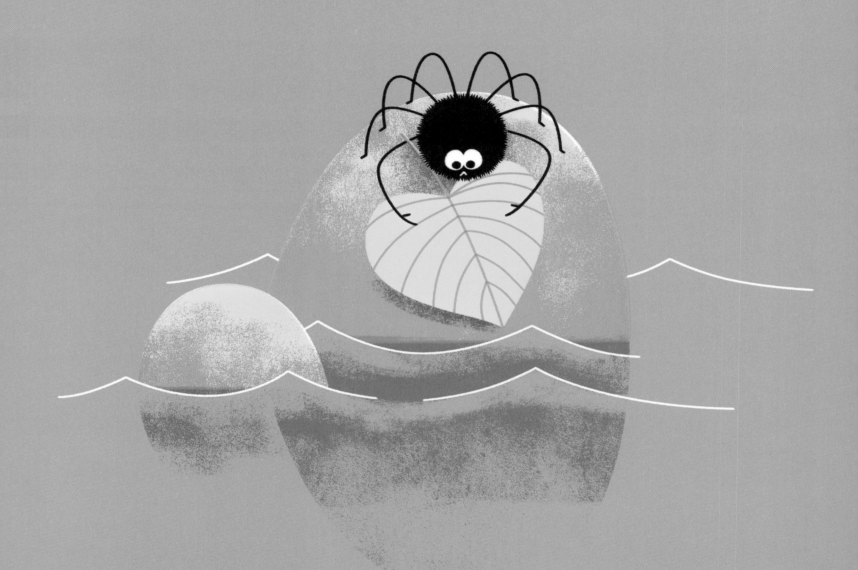

Though he ties it tightly...

the wind takes his last leaf away.

Stanley has lost everything.

Hasn't he?

He weaves through the night.

In the morning...

it is time for Stanley to
catch a lift on the wind again.